T0063557

Unto Relationship

A Short Primer of Twelve Essays

by
Elizabeth Clayton

Trafford rev. 03/27/2021

 www.trafford.com

North America & international
toll-free: 844-688-6899 (USA & Canada)
fax: 812 355 4082

Life is ought but the unfolding of
will and circumstance,
sentiment added to, and relationships
can unravel the self in their
interactions.

February 12, 2009
In deepest night
Elizabeth

Table of Contents

Foreword

It is an honor to write a foreword for someone such as Elizabeth Clayton. I have had the pleasure and honor to be her physician over the last several years. She has persevered with bipolar illness and done what very few have been able to do which is to use her malady as a source of insight and inspiration. Elizabeth is a woman who has lived life to the fullest and has experienced the entire spectrum of emotions from rapture to melancholia. I think that this circumstance combined with her artistic abilities and her courage and compassion allow her to be such a gifted and powerful writer. She has taught me more about love, about relationships and about embracing life that anyone I can remember.

Elizabeth has a passion for teaching and to see the excitement and energy that she has for instructing college students is a joy to behold. She is someone who out of her pain, her joy and life experiences can capture the passion of life in a unique and amazing way. I have been moved in reading her books and viewing her paintings and it has prompted me to examine my life more honestly. She is above all a real and genuine woman who is not judgmental and tries to meet others where they are in life and to enrich them. I am honored to be able to share with you my thoughts on this delightful and talented writer. I can only hope that she will continue to bless us with more projects so that we can see the world in new and exciting ways which she brings to life.

John Norton, M.D.

Acknowledgements

It is well and good to be gracious and appreciative when a project is completed, especially if those involved have reason to believe it to be a worthy task; usually several or many individuals do their part with the work required.

With this composition I acknowledge first and most my psychiatrist and friend Dr. John Norton at the University of Mississippi Medical Center in Jackson, Mississippi. He, as is his usual stance, searched through a basket of flowers to find an idea and held it out to me, a challenge that I needed in capturing the beauty of writing this piece, always, in every session, offering encouragement and praise. Words are simply inadequate in expressing appreciation for his acknowledgement of me and my work.

And then, standing by were Ora Steele, seeing that all clerical matters were kept in order, patient, encouraging, and efficient -- And, as well, my dear friend Lynn Waltman, who "wore a great many hats", to see the piece into publication, through hours of different industries.

As to readers, there was none other than Dr. Norton (for few even knew the small work was in progress) save one good friend: I offer sincere gratitude for his interest and helpful remarks.

We were a legion of five and have rolled the stone up the mountain once again – and so, great thanks, until the next time.

Elizabeth, August 10, 2009

Preface

Unto Relationship is a piece, a record, with interpretation, of accumulated naturalistic observations, the method used in the first attempts to study human behavior, other than reviewing man's expression of self and nature in art and literature. And still today, we cannot place human beings in cages, cells, or rooms to be observed and their behaviors recorded. Some variation on this arrangement exists but not as with primitive, lower animals – and there are shouts of protest, even when small rodents are used. Andso, in the twelve essays which comprise the work, (easily read in one sitting), are observations "in the natural," and the very personal insights gleaned of them over a period of years, beginning in my early adulthood, although there was much "face watching" as a child, so as to understand motivation and forthcoming behavior.

There are no studies or statistical findings recorded, for instruction and reading, presenting information to classes for nearly thirty years, together with my personal spectator guise at play, have superseded them. Harlow's studies, object relations theory, separation anxiety and the "invulnerables" (children of actively ill schizophrenics), with their findings are well known to me, with their wisdoms, as are the effects of the kibutzes and marasmus, "latch key" children, "time out" and successive approximation, independent and dependent variables, generally, and schedules of reinforcement alongside unconditional positive regard, "significant others" and closure, cognitive disorders and acting out – all filling the large reservoir of my fish and loaves, a covering of varietal stimulus – response relationships splashing all about. Even Itard's <u>The</u> <u>Wild</u> <u>Boy</u> <u>of</u> <u>Averyon</u> proved an interesting, if sympathetic, "first" longitudinal study.

But these were not my fare; I wished to present that which I personally perceived, as I moved through my days, of my fellows, to state such that the reader outside academia could comfortably peruse and benefit somewhat with new, very old wisdoms, perhaps better put, a kind of "fireside chat" experience, reviewing information which is of interest and importance to a great many.

The twelve essays which follow are from some of the observations which most interested me concerning human behavior in relationships. They may appear critical of relationship, but nonetheless show opportunities for meaningful physical and emotional interaction which are obviously necessary for the fullness of the human animal. We are gregarious creatures and seek out our own.

The self is paramount in the realm of existence, but within it is the capacity for much worthy sentiment and beautiful experience, with and among others. The paradoxical nature of man is the understatement, resting on the inconsistencies that are ours, each as we struggle with will and circumstance, toward a goal not well defined, for many, or certain for most.

– Wishing balm for those in problematic relationships, and a salute to those happily engaged: – Roses!

Elizabeth, March 22, 2009

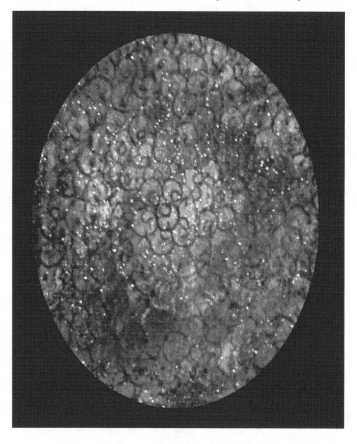

Beginnings

In the purely raw, we are, and most, islands unto ourselves – that is the way of beginning – so harsh the tearing of birth itself: noise and make-up are great conspirators, and for the most, accomplish, at least in part, their purposes. That is the reason for the continuous gathering of the garbage of noise; but the residual self, the self alone, left, is the integrity of person, his ennoblement manifesting in death and its non-directive, to all knowing, path, that sponsors no hands offering.

Relationship is, then, the essence of our striving, but away, in part, from our nature. To feel that we must osmose into another completely, permanently, is to farewell our noble human core.

There are respites along the path of any endeavoring, any effort, and we grasp them as eagerly, as joyfully as we may; and this behavior is good. But there would be no stars, no sun, no heaven, of whatever variety, to search for, to reach toward, to yearn in sweet pain, in wanting, if they were always present. The human heart must to have its emptinesses, the fallow ground in order to approach a prize, a reason to be, to yield a harvest, play out a melody: otherwise is wanton abundance where there are no parameters that define the ecstasy of the prize.

Ought, therefore, but to closet, to hide some portion of the self that it wait, to yearn, to prepare for the prize.

Elizabeth, January, 2009

Forward Steps, "Unto . . ."

Just as the forsythia in its bells of brightest yellow are nudging into the bitter January chill, words, phrases, ideas, through conversation, bend around the corners of my awareness – in these early hours, words in communion with my confessor, my mentor, my companion, my fullest presence. We speak of many things, and always of relationship, the word pounding in this, my fertile, silent conversation.

He has suggested that I pen my thoughts, and I have waited until they touched me with the strength of the muse – with the exception of some few beginning remarks, gathered together in an idle evening.

Andso, the pen – "relationship" is not a static word or concept, canoting motionlessness, or unproductive stillness, but rather, movement of some fashion, reaching about. It usually implies two individuals, in some kind of movement, but is a phenomenon that can include others beside. We are animals with humanity, and wish, almost as we fear, disclosure, to tell another. We seek to hold to our birthing vessel as long as we live, either literally or in some metaphorical maneuver, while more, for most, striving to pull away.

Perhaps freedom is our greatest need, for in it is the seed of self, from wherever it may have sprung. But this freedom requires an audience, a mirror, and we seek it in another, for our dependence has already been established. This activity is always sensual in coloring, for it excites and is pleasurable when the need is, indeed, for most, met, and to some degree, for a period, brief or extended, troubled or with ease – before decisions are made to remain or to dissolve and begin again.

It may be that relationship is a selfish arrangement, even with giving.

Partners, for their major purpose, are in place, at least in the beginning, for the purpose of revealing the self, yet an aggrandizement, as it were. During these early exchanges, giving is, for the greater part, for out of the arena of such behaviors. Oftentimes, the problem that emerges, within a period of some months or a year, is the calling out of the needing self, the fuller needing self, to be more, as suggested by the partner, something which was, at the first, an attracting characteristic, now an impossible requirement.

Not unusual is the expectation that both individuals wish the other to carry the relationship, provided attraction being sufficient for continuance (and this matter is entirely different from earlier ideas mentioned, to be addressed later); scripts have usually evolved and needs have begun to be met or not met – or since familiarity is a coin, dear, exchanges may continue past realization that the self is not being wombed and suckled, without, of course, the trappings of these such.

A relationship, one between two individuals, and just as truly between several persons, if continuing past a point in which familiarity offers convenience and comfortableness – it can remain in place, but a slow denouement often can also begin. It may be that someone new comes to a partner or that other circumstances occur, and often with struggle. At this time assessment begins, slowly or abruptly, as the stage offers, and the "giving" component in the relationship is stacked beside the embellishment of the self. A strong partner will exit, for the giving was, could not be enough in a seeking relationship of aggrandizement; a weaker partner will neurotically placate, for there are privileges in relationships, and sweet bondage. At other times when there are enough plans (to maintain appearances, not true feelings of fidelity), arrangements are sometimes put in place, and these people live to die and be buried beside each other.

The point is made, then, that, at least one motivation for relationship is the acknowledgement, yet celebration of self carried out by the "helping" partner, established early or not at all. It is altogether possible that consummate love (care) can develop within these boundaries, its reality depending on many variables which will require a discussion, full and inclusive of human qualities that elude "parlor" thought.

Elizabeth
February 2009

Ebbing and Tiding

In recent days a knowing has come under my conscious eye regarding a matter of great interest to me: the activity of others with me and around me – couples, dyads, triads, these with groups including larger numbers of others, and singles. These relationships are, generally, on-going, even with large periods of time when there are few, or no exchanges. But the troth is kept, in small ways such as observing special days, with events involving family and friends, yet at times isolated, spontaneous "happenings." An ebbing and tiding of behaviors and feelings, even with frequent interactions, is, however, always in place. The forward movement between "partners" of a relationship may be a shifting, an intensification, or a diminishing, but the individuals involved are as if they are in the activity of dancing, coming together, to pull apart, to come back together again – or to change to another partner or remain more isolated, to rest.

It may be that there is a "testing" after a show of dependence in the need and enjoyment of a relationship, a testing of commitment and loyalty. Often small misunderstandings that call for apology, or long silences following an act or event require a re-expressing of the need to be together; a declaration, in some manner, that the relationship is more important than before this recent examination, can occur.

These episodes most often make the relationship stronger, although some alterations will have been put in place. There is a gentle paranoia that is "free-floating" among those who disclose, and these skirmishes are, in the general, healthy. However, as we grow more into the people we really are, the individuals we are programmed and shaped by experience to be, alterations sometimes include a gradual drifting away into a cessation of contact and communication. The relationship is placed in yesterday, in memory, not bitter necessarily or sorrowful, but simply accepted as part of the movement of our lives; more, external variables can intervene causing a different scenario, but usually such a circumstance is prologued by the scene described before – and there are re-ignitings of feelings and needs following a circumstance which comes after a long absence of relationship: chemistry, shared goals and past experiences, proximity, individual maturing and growth, (including the expansion of interests and philosophical stance) – all are some of the factors which come together to bind or break. It really does not matter if the relationship is sensual, fraternal, obligatory, service or other – these factors stated do interact together, with others, and the ebbing and tiding make the particular ambiance, the personality of the extant relationship.

It is as if we are all, each, basically insecure, covered or not, and need new reinforcement from our partners, on often occasions, that shows we are necessary, in some part, for their full happiness and content, therefore giving us the acknowledgement and acceptance we need to be our full selves.

– Regarding the presence of basic insecurity: it is a growing awareness that as children we have little concern with, if all other matters and issues are in proper arrangements. We play, filling and passing our hours with whomever is around, in quite uncomplicated recipes, their coming and going not even an idea entertained. But as we mature, in thought, particularly, our needs change, increasing in intensity, selectivity, and movement, among and with others. It may be that the powerful nineteenth century German poet, Holderlin, was correct in his assessment of man's growing sense of the becoming dilemma of his ephemeral nature, stating "Man is the only animal who knows that someday he will die." This is a difficult, a heavy realization, and we look for someone to help shoulder it: relationship becomes the antidote to incompleteness, fear, and ultimate despair, the strength we must add to our own consciousness and will.

One characteristic of the ebbing and tiding of relationship is the play of tense following a breach, questioning, fatigue – or many other interrupting factors/circumstances; the longer the period between the pulling away and initiative to come back together, the more likely a re-uniting will not occur, or it is more difficult to effect. The initial movement is more often in the behavior of the partner who has always "carried" the relationship; if this is not the pattern, domination or power assertion may be at work, although spontaneous, fresh claspings do burst forth with effort by both partners out circumstances as complex as human nature allows.

Elizabeth – In deepest night

Fabric

A thread that runs throughout the fabric of relationship, somewhat negative but very often seen, is the use of a partner to support in the face of self doubt, that is, one partner playing the "devil's advocate." Doubting one's own attitudes, strengths, intimacies can be very painful and when we are in close fellowship with another, baring our almost whole selves, the occasion to view our partner's insecurities or hearing troubling expressions very often presents itself. Instead of giving support to the openly needy partner, one partner will, at times, join the ranks of the aggressor or spend great effort to present his position positively, citing his (openly needing partner) qualities that enter the troubled situation which have caused the discordant behavior, leaving the disturbed partner to feel that he misperceives, has impure motives, does not have sufficient information or any of many other stances which leave him concluding that he is "in the wrong" rather than the often obviously apparent position of being wronged.

This is a puzzling circumstance, but very likely it gives the partner who plays the "advocate" a sense of control, that he is directing, in some fashion, the thought and behavior of the dance macabre of a small portion of humanity.

It seems that a feeling of complete acceptance of the disturbed partner is present, or a great dependence on the part of this person in distress so that there is no fear of rejection of the pressed partner who asks for support: confession equals subordination, the treachery of openness.

It may be that simply voicing a situation in which unpleasantries exist suggests to the partner who is presently without conflict that he is, happily, given an opportunity to stand a bit taller, his wisdom having been invited, suggesting strength he may wish to possess; and so he will set matters in balance at the expense of the now more needy partner.

Such is unhealthy motivation and shows a weakness in the fabric of the relationship if it is purported to be one full and whole, in which partners have equal station/position. Sado-masochistic tendencies work off each other, if they are successful – and even the keenest perception may envision only active competition; and it could be a part of the pattern, but the motivation, whether of a visiting nephew, a girlfriend, one's lover or whomever, is to build up by planting doubt, thusly making weak something once stronger – all in the guise of the wise good. The "advocate" wishes all to think as he and cannot understand this iron position or even approach realization of his motives.

Literature, including case histories, cite simple denial, avoidance, or expressing "not understanding" being used to cast the necessary doubt in the needy partner's mind, as to the awkwardness of his behaviors or the ineptness of his expressions. Individuals play out this script for years, through the entire relationship, as doubt is repeatedly suggested and reinforced, causing an eroding of confidence and selfhood into more dependence in a situation in which strength is taken in exchange for another's self worth.

Great frustration is felt in this unhappy pantomime, especially when some strength is still present in the openly dependent partner. Three interesting, recurring dreams have been reported as occurring for years during such a circumstance: uncontrollable pulling down of all draperies in the household; extracting reams and reams of stripped flax out one's mouth, and more obviously stating the partner's felt dilemma at not being supported but verbally "losing" in the skirmish – tying and gagging the "advocate" and expressing the "whole truth," the reality of the circumstance, giving forth his "word-hoard," as it were.

Elizabeth -- In deepest night
February 12, 2009

Egocentricity

Egocentricity can sometimes be an advantage, all too often in a sensationalistic culture. Being intelligent, "overmuch," and "different" (an adjective used often to refer to special abilities and some other qualities, marginal), may still conjure up evaluations which are negative, but not so much so as in past years. Social movements, a broadening of general education and its accompaniments, specific events, historically – all have helped to ease the hardship the "Jones" have, in the past, placed on many. Indeed there has grown up a pseudo-appreciation for genius and talent; its greatest flaw and the quality that places it in a "pseudo" category is that the appreciation is directed at easy identity and fashionable recognition.

In truth, we might safely surmise that today, in most progressive cultures, the absurd is often touted as the acceptable, however much pain may rest in the heart. Andso, mutual experiences and other minuses call together many who reinforce each other's identifying, but limited, more bittersweet components which draw their person. These "partners" emerge an island in a sea of what they perceive as alienation and they cling to each other for there appears no ready respite. Psychotherapy has become pharmacologically dependent, and souls who have some insight within their loneliness could benefit from cathartic directiveness but cannot find either enough ego strength to embark or a worthy and able mentor to guide. They continue in a half miserable, half elitist fashion with the rewards such an arrangement can offer. Their dependence on each other can be restrictive regarding each other's possible improvement and increase competition that will "prove" a "healthy", more safe, balance. In the layman's world, which is most of it, attractiveness alongside ableness often knells deadly, for "no one" other than the partner (and competition may have become a factor) wants to dance with a ballerina.

Elizabeth -- In deepest night
February 12, 2009

Inconsistencies

A very unattractive, problematic arrangement among people, generally, but in more strongly fixed relationships, is inconsistency – that of the "active" partner which is put in place, he only to exhibit behavior, and offer expressions, ideas, over and again, as if the receiving partner does not, indeed, perhaps, cannot see or remember. Often to save a relationship, for any number of reasons, the dependent partner (receiving) will absorb these condesentions, a slight of some magnitude. Rationalization of factors that are involved and the contrived manner in which they are instituted is often reached for so that there exists "peace at all cost."

This circumstance has always been found, moreso among female partners, in earlier times, since so few opportunities for "breaking out" were available. Often, if one did change her position, it was to a similar, if somewhat kinder situation.

Today, however, the problem is still prevalent, the stage and props merely changed, or new confusion added. Sexual indiscretions are more widely accepted, loyalty and honor hardly known concepts; irresponsibility and unfaithfulness abound, without censor, past the revealing. These undesirable qualities are still woven into relationships and are allowed or condoned for many similar (as earlier) and different reasons – and oftentimes the "cost" is selfhood – of a partner, a child, an acquaintance, a potential partner – almost in any relationship; a hollow shell is more truly a shell than such interaction, a "relationship."

February 12, 2009
Elizabeth -- In deepest night

Braggadocios

Braggadocios catch attention and frequently can hold their audience until some interactive bonds are established, often if the "partner" has deficiencies which are significant and comes to enjoy more confidence because "someone," yet an aggressive companion, shadows the perceived inadequacies which he feels allow him no partner at all.

This feat is accomplished through lineage, acreage (financial holdings), education, profession, interactive skills and appearance. And these arrangements, once established, are not pure, but mixed as to traits and genuine good feelings that develop together with those that also, ultimately, diminish.

Routines and expectancies find schedules, especially when some period of time in relationship has passed; even recognition of the smallnesses and inadequacies simply make conclusions difficult, if not impossible – though in actuality, theoretical players could, more, should be moved to better positions. But life is not a game of chess, however much it resembles the entire process, and our humanity requires certain amounts of nourishment, pawns that we may become to receive it.

Braggadocios come in all colors and forms and truth comes, usually, with intimacies, but the pattern is already established and reinforcements are scheduled. The "nudge" maneuver is then often used – suggesting and offering credentials that make the braggart (who may not appear always so much so). He may don a silent, secretive, distantly superior stance, with conversation and activities that dress him as "above" and good, a superlative physical self with added saintliness, appealing to many, if not scrutinized. The braggart comes easily to intimidate his partner with his piety and efiteness as well as through his more aggressive manner, his force and charm. His partner, then, indulges him, unless a matter of some import is in question. We live, as partners, all, with the grey malaise of apathy, or perhaps simply because we have no "cause" with the current trivialization of so many of our holdings, despite the noise made concerning which end of the egg is proper to break (Swift close here).

In this charade, none of the partners are fulfilled: there are those who must be "pumped up" and those who must "pump"; there is not worthiness in either.

Elizabeth -- In deepest night
February 12, 2009

The Seeker

The English poet, Robert Browning, identified a problematic partner in relationships, indirectly, in Pippa, a little girl who was employed in housekeeping, but on her day off wanted only "God in His heaven, all right with the world." Gender aside, large numbers of individuals only want their worlds "right"; just to be heard, to be acknowledged, to share interests outside the norm are enormous calling cards to some who wish giving relationships. "The seeker" looks with patience, often over and again, quite willing to repair "the rest" if some can be found – no matter that "baggage" equally, or more, is present also.

"Trying," overmuch, for the crumbs – being open, honest, fair, being strong – on somewise can be a trap. Add the pervasive Judeo – Christian sentiment as well as that illicited by the whole of nature, simple with complex reasoning, being careful to listen, beside special sensibilities – and yielded is the Pippa partner: vulnerable to the activity of partners borrowing off each other, quickly using up great portions of the "all right" and not being able to repair "the rest." Dependencies and expectations are established to be serviced out of weaknesses inside disillusionment, guilt, and a growing ennui.

Elizabeth -- In deepest night
February 12, 2009

Friendships

"A man needs two things in life to be happy: a person to love and a work to love:"

-- a friend, Standly, diagnosed Paranoid Schizophrenic, in a period of recent remission --

A phenomenon I find interesting in relationships, one that is more recently seen, particularly in the years following the sixties decade, when friendship supplanted almost all other important values, is the tendency today for "partners" in relationships to play roles that are similar/equal and those, particularly, young now, mutual sexual entities. They call each other "friends" and contend that erotic feelings have no place in the relationship, even if their "partners" are oppositely gendered.

Selfhood has become the grail to achieve out the philosophical bramble of the four decades since the sixties, a new type of humanism, seated in an egalitarian realm that is surpassing all other personal qualities. It is not a long or involved thought which carries one to the dilemma of identity becoming a more difficult process, longer to achieve, than it has been in the past, for most young people, yet extending into each age-stage.

Many cohorts enter the establishing of identity in present times, and a very popular point of arrival is not now often heard, the resonating words of Biff in the sixties' play "Death of a Salesman" by A. Miller: "I know who I am." And not playing masculine and feminine roles that are well drawn almost supersedes the anatomical prologuing of this circumstance. The Vietnam War, throughout the sixties; the feminist movement following; the Civil Rights movement before (in this country), clearly underscoring the equality of all persons; the entire field of Psychology absolutely raising the development of self, (a prescription self), to gigantic proportions in its literature and influence – these all have effected a mentality of sameness in which models do not have enough differentiating features to fully allow a child to choose gender-specific perceptions and behaviors.

Added to these factors is the trivialization of sex to the extent that many young people think of a relationship that is wholesome to be one without erotic qualities; those are left to necessary, but less desirable, partners (in all areas other than sexual stimulation).

What has emerged is a fraternal perception of "relationship" no matter that gender is still a reality. Opposite sexed relationships are placed in the same category as those same sexed. Activities include partners that are "just friends" and group gatherings cause inclusion in which the individual is secondary, and other arrangements are very popular, as well as objectification to many offerings: profession, money; causes, all is avant guard as possible; business that serves as a rouse for creativity, or weighing ingenuine hard honesty and raw frankness as positive personal attributes.

These factors collectively, have resulted in a casualness which gives less attention to gender specific behaviors such as grooming and dress that heighten suggestibility, leaving more needed energy to intellectual pursuits – however, quite without a requiring balance. These micro-behaviors, children of the dragon, "progress," have added problematic confusion while not completely dismantling the former norm, a stance which only further adds to the existing confusion. It is not unusual, at all, today, to see a communicant in cut-offs and sneakers approach the altar to receive the Eucharist from a priest in full dress regalia, silver chalice beside. Such is a confusion of signals, one of many that permeates our culture. Paradoxical instruction is helpful, but, moreso, if cushioned by strong consistency as well. As Hebb has written, the brain requires a certain amount of organization to properly function.

Being masculine and feminine, even with hormones and a culture which exploits being one or the "other," makes young people, and those older, also, afraid to try to fulfill their needs, establish a firmly distinguishable gender identity, or all other qualities which are identity centered.

"Partners," then, today suffer from a lack of commitment, commitment born of healthy intimacy and completeness, and they feign relationships that are intense without this needed quality, left, in place, comfortable relationships, that quality alone. This situation involves opposite sexed partners, but extends into same sex relationships. In the residue there occurs poorly developed gender development "in the round," and often individuals do not know, with security, how to conduct their actions and behaviors with many others.

"Friends" are necessary and good, those male and female, a statement full and true, but there is a closeness to deficiency today, in this culture, in the continuing insisting of sameness, equality, traditional non-erotic exchanges and other similar behaviors which allow distanced relationships that result in the overuse of the phone, computers, cell phones, cameras, etc., "groupie mania" acceptance of sexual identities that are confused (to the point of promoting such) and/or mixed, and simply put, near a knowing, in which individuals are frightened to play out roles that are different, if equal.

The result is a loneliness, a lack of security, exuberance and creativity, intimacies that feed and, together, give strength, and support that hold the soul; and an almost fashionable blending of selfhood is occurring, it into "en masse" where there is little responsibility to act as an individual, however much this circumstance began with the idea of the celebration of the individual. The movement has, to a symptomatic degree, gone awry and partners align with others as children on a playground, not accepting life in its reality, but rather "playing" at it – a fancy: safer, but in relationships that are more empty, or better put, not complete enough for true fulfillment, perhaps some of the reason for the cloud of ennui that covers our people.

Without sufficient certainty, expectations, responsibility and commitment we are left with misgivings, regrets, isolation or alienation, and loneliness – full, consummate love close by, only in thought perusal and reflection.

Consider -- Chinua Achebe, the celebrated twentieth century, Nigerian novelist on balance/interdependence: "Extremes carry the seeds of destruction – between earth and sky, individual and community, man and woman," or different perspectives on the same situation. Igbo thought is fundamentally that of dualistic thought; "Nothing is absolute: ...a balance must be achieved."

Elizabeth
February 12, 2009

The Self

To address the subject of relationship without giving some good amount of attention to the self and its intraexchanges would be like making oatmeal cookies at Christmas and leaving out the oatmeal. Something would emerge from the oven, but it would be without proper identity. Oatmeal is a fairly easily obtainable ingredient, but the self, for observation and study, has been, always, even before full consciousness, as we understand it, evolved – when primitive man dug into his own flesh and screamed into the elements – the self has remained clothed, couched, veiled – in mystery, from the first moment of its recognition as a construct: elusive, obscure, allthewhile calling to reason and the senses.

For many it is, and remains, constant, always, a shadowed part of one's nature, one that he plans to "get to" someday, but conveniently conjures up enough noise, entangles himself in enough circumstance and bramble that the time of "getting to it," does not ever become appropriate for proper scrutiny; we accept easy scripts, allow the trivial to surround and impinge on us so that our final response is a sigh that the "world" is just "too much with us ...".

With others, the self is a problem that invites attention at different levels, it being given some time and reflection – at holidays, funerals, when the seasons change or on the occasion of a broken relationship. These can be difficult hours and often some good, productive work is done, but intensive study, in time, gives over, in various guises, to the routines of our lives, the seemingly necessary matter of "adjusting." More alert, appropriate affect returns, as does tone of voice, and focus – to listening, away from the becoming, once more, distant self, leaving a foundation, still less than sound, for relationship.

And then there are those who, with full courage and true variegations in strength, approach the quest of self in a more intense and methological fashion. They stand in the face of this knowing: to itself, the "self" is a paradoxical entity: open to close, security atop insecurity; placid stances to give over to torrents of feelings; we seek the familiar, sameness, consistency, but thrill to the unusual, the unique, the rare and select. But "relation," in a word means "telling" unto kinship, and so how do we become partners without knowing what to express or "tell"; clearly to be in relationship is to know one's self that it be made bare to another and this act in turn reciprocated.

It is difficult to examine one's trousers while one is wearing them. Simple observation is possible, yielding knowledge of color, texture, and lines, but not a great deal more is accomplished – and so with the self: when one is at the point of ableness in "knowing" himself, he is already "it" – "it" is I, me, and looking outside "to see what we see," from the inside, becomes a truly arduous task. But until this task is at least mostly, or partially accomplished, our relationships will embark as unstable skiffs in difficult waters.

To begin, then, we approach the paradoxical element the self is: it is the fountainhead, in all of its pluses and minuses, to understanding the difficulty of the quest for isness, and it is also a springboard to many attending realizations. We are, and we are not. We have our physical self, or our perception of it, including gender and other qualities; and we have thought, reason, and the chest which houses the seeds of our sensual, creative, and spiritual selves. We are, then, and we are not – we are physical beings, within physical properties and boundaries, and, are not, by the lines of the absences our thoughts and needs draw.

Interwoven throughout the fabric of the self are the very legions of variables over which we have no control before maturity, and many that manifest, outside our constraints, after physical maturation. We do not choose, nor can we modify, our parents, nor the cohorts of time and place of our lives: as to record, the plains of Carthage, fallen, were setting to Patton only once.

We do have the power of adaptation and can adjust to a great many factors/ circumstances, but the "self" is already mostly in place when we recognize that adjustments must occur. Open to us, then, in summary, to share with our "partners" is no more than acceptance: gracefully or not, with faith or without; with rejection, even rebellion; with yearning, and resignation, stoically or with fatigue. In these lie the oatmeal of the cookie.

In all likelihood, these "oatmeals" abide, in different denominations, in all of us, one or another being dominant, it giving the force that empowers the qualities which are inside and the manner in which they manifest. Eastern thought has suggested, in all of its wisdom, that we quieten the rise of the oatmeal, that we then somehow reach the level of self at which it is no longer extant, but immersed in the whole of "things"– all energy in peaceful unison. This idea is foreign to the vitality of nature, of which we are part, separate but compatible, else destroyed or refashioned. Erotic energy is necessary to life, do as we will, once in it, but nature teaches lessons the self can learn at any age-stage and accompanying complexion. It offers the innocence of the child, the tenderness of the petal, the purity of water, the passionate intensity of the rarest ruby, the fierceness of fire, the rage in wind and pain in lightening – to soften into the grace of the rainbow, and in constancy of seasons, the devotion of the saints: this, the stage for we lesser Gods, to tryst with that real, and not in an academic milieu.

The great paradox, then, hangs about as a magnificent veil: light and dark, sun and moon, life and death, warmth and cold, pleasure and abstinence; growth and harvest shout out green and gold, and the radiance that leads to winter's chill is enhanced by short hours to recollection.

These principles must come to be accepted in the self, each in its particular dress, so that security be achieved, not just from death, but from the many conclusions, happenchances, mishaps, yet losses of the everyday.

Reason is to be assessed – its boundaries alongside special aptitudes that can flower and give flavor to one's inner larder: being able in selective areas, and most are, if only in interest and instruction, can cause a blooming, a meadowing, a pasture and garden for the spirit – all gifts to exchange with "partners."

And then the matter of passion – it does not pale in acceptance – the rainbow arcs masterfully after the storm; as Zorba says, "Every man needs a little madness": – the impetus for the shoot, the bud, the first light of day to spread, like a man over a woman.

These pursuits lead indirectly to spiritual and creative seeds, stored in thought, gathered of innate sensibilities, experience, and instruction. These avenues need must to be recognized and cultivated for they are the breath of true life, the woodland spring, flowered of creekside violets, nearby or swimming gracefully, tassels from abundant greens: thallo, lime, chartreuse, empire and fern – these into immortality, through death and refashioning.

To accept one's physical self inside its physical boundaries, one's capacity to do and feel – the entire spectrum – to lift out, and to pull from within himself expression of his appreciation of life – with its inconsistencies, darkness, complexities and ironies (including physicality gone awry), is man/woman to stand crown of nature, the reflection of it, it the face of God, in His ever saga of amusement: passion and resting.

Noted is that no instructive steps or documented studies have been given, to be followed, that will facilitate seeing the "whole" trousers while wearing them, no objectives that will assure ready assessment as we step into the expanses of vocational, or sensual pleasure, and as importantly, creative and spiritual holdings – or that sprinklings over one's self will not be showers of indecision, confusion, and melancholy. But to recognize the fundamental aspects of the self, as they indeed, are, and to act on the strength of these insights is to present to a "partner" as much truth as possible; and as an old maxium states – "there is always enough in what is left."

Socrates merely said it; "knowing" oneself, the oatmeal, is not a collection of facts, tenets, postulates, a prepared writ; it is in the always reflection of what is perceived in the moment, and accepting, or rejecting . . ., whatever leaves peace in the inner chambers of the person manifest. All do so, to some extent, in this fashion, and their relationships reflect their recipe.

Elizabeth

March 15 – 16, 2009

Boundaries

Most people think of a boundary as being an outer marking, points or a point which serve(s) as a designation of size, position, utility. Everything on the inside of the marker is recognized in a special way of correctness, acceptability; everything beyond is looked upon in a variety of ways which indicates exclusion. While physical boundaries concept most easily to us, it is those within that wield much more power, having the strength of thought and reason. It is they that are more likely to offer problems in navigation, whether the traversement be physical or mental.

In relationships, "partners" bring a mixed salad of boundaries, these to be dealt with by them personally, and also by their companion partner or partners. It is altogether possible that within these boundaries lie the life of the relationship, for many are fixed, intractable and impossible with which to negotiate. Others may be more pliable and malleable, and most all of the exchanges can be accomplished.

Physical boundaries that enter into the success or failure of relationship, or perhaps just the degree of comfortableness, contentment, growth – joy – are very familiar to us, including such factors as material goods, physical attractiveness, intelligence, and health. These being in place help greatly in allowing one to seek out companionship and enable him to engage a partner or partners. Non-physical boundaries, however, are more subtle in their appearances, and often an exchange may have been begun and be in progress when they, like a shadow at eventide, slowly begin to etch into the dynamics of the relationship. Perhaps the partner with the problem boundary is unaware of it, or has played out the scenario before, hoping "this time" he can accomplish his goals. He may begin compatibly at first, and in a kind of confabulation, try different strategies, deny that a problem exists, or simply withdraw without explanation; or it may be that the current stronger "partner" has qualities which illicit from his companion "partner(s)", unworkable responses in the longterm.

If enough time, effort and feeling have already been given to the relationship, truth may be searched out and communication will facilitate the continuance of the relationship. These communications can be difficult, and a multitude of attending variables contribute to the outcome: past experiences, other activities and partners, (as relief valves), and simply fatigue. Often professional counseling is included with multiple self-help stratagems.

The reason for inner boundary problems being more difficult to solve is that they are, most, seated in a powerfully negative psychological area: the realm of the emotion of fear: the fear may be the result of instruction/learning, experience, or innate sensibilities and temperament. The source does not matter so much as does the manifestation. Andso, we have those who, with great need, wish relationship, but are unable to sustain one at all or only a small number that are satisfactory which are not at a distance. Some "push on through" and "make the relationship work," but, then, there is sacrifice.

We wear our fears as we do our clothes: different styles for different people. At times great effort is not required, while at others, the full wardrobe is brought out. There is the partner, who draws the line at true intimacy, or at commitment and responsibility; the factor of control or narcissistic needs may be at work, and there are those who do not want to deal with family, matters of faith and other similar factors. And there are those who erect barriers by competing, by using a conglomerate of methods, or manipulating to advantage. It may be that matters of esteem, unfortunate past experiences, family models and instruction, gender ambivalence, sensitivity overmuch or a kind of elitism born of perceived or true inadequacies, with many faces, foundation, either separately or some together, these sources of fear. Poor mental and/or physical health, especially poor emotional health, can foster many of these problem areas since it so often manifests in less than desirable social skills, communication being the vehicle of relating.

The matter is rather like that of the act of rape: there really are fewer than greater numbers of these experiences, for both partners know at an early juncture where particulars lie – likeso with boundaries in relationships. If couples, friends, acquaintances have been in fellowship long enough for a strong fear to be illicited, an event will call out a labeling. One or both partners was expecting the encounter, and its assessment and resolution will depend on the strength of the fear, past experiences, the degree of involvement already in place and present needs with selected other circumstances particular to the exchange. Thusly, "all things being equal," a partner does not "just" lose interest; a relationship does not "just suddenly go bad"; and one partner does not "just" outgrow another.

A brief concluding statement might properly be made: relationships do continue for many years, lifetimes, when unwanted boundaries exist between the partners. There might have been a bright beginning, but as truth would out, there is, in reality, a long "falling action," unfulfilling, devoid of any of the first blush. One is too weak to go, one to have him/her go. This arrangement is found often among couples, but among longtime friends, acquaintances and relatives.

There are many Hamlets: they are not all royalty, nor do they choose to exit honorably.

Elizabeth
March 18, 2009

Seasons

There is an ambiance of soft poignancy about the concept, the word, "seasons"; as soon as it is spoken or read, it breathes a sigh, one of longing with one of quiet resignation. Perhaps in our culture it is most associated with special times of festival or periods of the life cycle symbolized by the coming and progress of the unfolding tense of the calendar. Joy and youth are celebrated sentiments, as are, truthfully, their passing, beside the traditions that then surround them.

Like the first glimpse of daybreak, or the last glimmer of twilight, the glint of a sword, the giving smile, we look upon this word in quiet wonder – and most probably would not associate it with the subject of relationships, but "relationship," in truth, is a season, brief, or of some length, and more importantly – there are "seasons" within extended relationships, the dividing into portions the special times which mark our hours. Perhaps most of the poignancy is felt in the canoting of conclusion when we concept the word. It is an immediate suitor to the beginning, which will, of course, win the hand.

When "partners" come together in relationship – long, dear friendships, respectful, loving familial exchanges, or the passionate caring interaction of the romantically involved – there is a kind of hunger in the first "days," a wish to not ever conclude, and many do not, throughout the script of natural law, but there do occur many shorter "seasons" within the whole, or at times, a rupture of the full relationship that is not ever restructured.

There are reasons, circumstances, situations – one might say "steps in the path" (for life has often been referenced as a journey), which contribute to the length or brevity of the seasons of our relationships. Some are a "normal" part of living, while others are not. For many, the concluding outcome of a relationship is as a primitive sentiment, on romantic love, written in one of my classes, some few years ago:

When you love some(one) so

deeply,
less they pass away,
the heart
is so heavy,
you wish that (he) (would) have
stayed.

Student comment late summer, 2001
Virginia College at Jackson, MS
English Composition, One

Relationships blaze as in the fury of raging fire, and endure, but also plateau into ambivalence and dissonance, a long quieting, a normally expected closing, or a complete cleavage without further association: there is the departing of childhood and innocence, the initial, and often, full disclosure in fraternity, the radiant passion of romantic love (Eros), the acceptance of the "real," "complete" individual in any relationship, as difficult as it may sometimes be – these all are seasons within relationships in which individuals are pressed to look at their partners – and themselves, and choose their responses.

Partners, whether sensual or otherwise, almost always remain in relationships, those that are satisfying, when certain factors or influencing variables are present: proximity, a commonly held, basic weltanschauung, similar education and background (family traditions, religion and others) good self esteem (especially the capacity for the respect of individual worth and growth); appreciation and its attending qualities which include thoughtfulness and acceptance of the unique; mutual goals and interests (rearing children, establishing in the work place [a profession], personal expression [creating], taking social responsibility, and working toward greater spiritual awareness).

Stated should be the principle that whoever the players, whatever the circumstances, relationship requires both spontaneity and contrived effort to remain viable, and within these avenues of behavior, a full portion of truth and justice, yielding the greatest fulfillment, as in Shakespeare's instruction in the tragicomedy, The Merchant of Venice; with these qualities present in all partners is found greatest conjugal, fraternal, and familial contentment although arrangements of pseudo – satisfaction do exist, many of them, but they are at risk, always – to an introduction, a reversal, an illness, an introspective experience.

Partners in relationships fare more poorly when other factors enter the exchange. Chemistry, now explored and studied, does play a role in the attraction process between partners, especially those sensual, but it is not enough, alone of others, to sustain longterm arrangements of fullness and productivity; attractiveness left unattended, whether of grooming, manners, or a lack of reciprocal behaviors with increasing expectations (even if suggested by the more giving partner in the earlier portion of the relationship) can grow to have a grave negative valence that shadows, to a degree, what was once brighter; eventually, the dragon of familiarity, too convenient security, together with the entering into other relationships or "arrangements," can prove problematic.

As partners grow more accepting with each other, too much intimacy in which needed "secrets" of selfhood are given over, a too strong a merging of a partner's centras can become a true, fundamental weakness in the "giving" structure. Growing as an individual, in awareness of one's place in the full flow of life, remaining fluid rather than static in thought, in the main, still requires some control and we cannot enjoy fullest "rapture" when a completely egalitarian stance is taken – throughout the relationships. This is not a conflicting statement: it does not soften truth; we must simply be true also to ourselves while not hurting another. One must feed his own soul, should it require a different food, at times, from his partner.

This circumstance comes to the fore, often after some years of relationship, as with couples when there is a setting aside of the "Cinderella" myth or whomever had been silently hoped a partner would become in maturity; with friends and family when losses, as with mental or physical health, occur, or perhaps a catastrophic event such as the death of a child. Egalitarianism in very intimate, longterm relationships is more a grooming process than an ideal to be achieved.

One's weltanschauung (basic life philosophy) comes under scrutiny with the arriving of a more definite facing of the hard reality of mortality, one's own mortality, the then weighing of the past, and fearing, at least having some degree of angst, about the future, especially if there is left work to be done with guilt, honor, devotion, and their all trappings. Friendships may become bothersome, a burden, or at best, distant; family and extended kin may appear more and more "out of step" and "demanding," or else more dear in the face of coming loss; couples may come to feel estranged from each other while caught up in personal dilemmas of significance, worth, and faith, and acknowledgement. One need only read the work of the sixteenth century English poet, John Donne, for record of such strivings. His great need to find fulfillment in sensual and spiritual realms, in the same relationship, tortured his days. It is difficult to be as another poet, of opposite disposition, Robert Browning, who embraced all of life, with vigor – love and work – into death. However, happily, in these strivings, "pearls at great price" are possible.

Partners in relationship, or with holding on to that which is not now present, must look at their seasons, as in all facets of life and juxtapose terms such as "forever," "always," "into eternis," or "an eon or two," or a remembered melody such as "MacArthur Park" – with a sigh, an echo, a halo, a fading dream – or, more constructively, with an histoire of doings and sayings: fruit that continues, surely, to ripen into every coming summer's visit, toward full isness in the glory of the season of mortality, at the harvest, with the smile of infinite Being.

Elizabeth -- In deepest night
March 20 – 21, 2009
Finished about 8 o'clock am

Into Relationship

Deep violet thoughts left the night,
opening the door to awareness,
and I knew in this octaved moment
that I was pardoned of my fashioning,
my condition of unlevenness;
and I was caught
in the strength of the scroll of His
winds,
in the care of His raindrop
of the cruel, heated summer,
in the moonfire of early morning
casting a mystery of an abundant
dawn.
The rare pungence of the early
hyacinth
poured out a natural blessing,
and I,
in my aloneness,
was covered with grace,
in the feathers and freedom of a
magnificent bird,
to come into relationship.

Elizabeth, Undated

An Elizabeth Afterthought

Upon finishing my small remarks on some aspects of the subject of relationship, occurring is the thought, the surfacing knowledge, that while there may be a good portion of reality presented, there are many out of relationship, and not because of any of the circumstances discussed, or more true, because of any circumstance, save their own personal desire, for a variety of reasons, to experience life as a solitary individual, solely, except within an I—Thou fellowship and perhaps nature; whatever the fashioning of this arrangement, it requires all energy and devotion, yielding a kind of beauty, while not rejecting others, but wishing to experience them through the devotional relationship.

This scenario can offer up much good, without intimacy and its entanglements, allowing contentment and fulfillment without a great of degree of disclosure. The monastic or ascetic avenues can or will be the correct course in daily living for selective personalities.

> "What did that nightingale not tell me? And how much did I say to it in silence." p. 32 ll. 6-7

> "And although you devote yourself in prayer to your fellow men, you remain unknown to

all men, and perhaps they will never know you." p. 33 ll. 6-8

"Whenever I had a strong desire to go to the desert, I would make myself experience the desert wherever I was." p. 49 ll. 23-25

From Elder Porphyrios in his autobiography, <u>Wounded</u> <u>by</u> <u>Love</u> – a Greek monk and priest who died in 1991 –

Addendum

Style/Worksheet

This exercise is a new genre in writing for me in that thinking consciously is superlative to expressing feeling spontaneously. I want to be informative about my subject, objective – shall we say – more academic within my physical round rather than freely emoting. It is enjoyable in a different fashion, but I miss my metaphors and symbols, juxtapositions, more graceful, full insights and descriptive outbursts. Others would be more positive toward me, spend more time with me, individually, if I tried to think, and express, in this manner more of the time – rather than letting my thoughts billow up into color and fancy, even if truth is tucked into some portion of the piece. I think people are, in the general, mundanely concrete, and I truly do not, nearly always, have control over the written expression of my spontaneous thought, so often emerging into consciousness from that great reservoir beneath where the feast is fully enjoyed.

– But I wish to "say" "some things," and some are more acceptable not said in verse; I will try to remember that the "reader" (customer) is always right!

Elizabeth, February 13, 2009

In deepest night after transcribing these portions, composed the night before, to be enlarged into perhaps a full prose piece –

Brainstorming

Relationship and association
Relationship and dependency
Spiritual oneness without boundaries
Appreciation
Competition
Complimenting colors
Absence and presence
Sensual flowering, coming later than initial
    attraction, infatuation
Convenience and security
Relationships and intelligence
Relationships and models
Relationships and chemistry (duration)
Relationship and fear
Relationship and core identity, to become
Relationship as abandonment of self
    (religious orders, causes)
Relationships and limitations
Relationships: to augment/compliment
Relationship resulting from ulterior motives
    of complex nature, (conscious/
    unconscious) – impet with sincerity,
    excitement, but ultimately
    metamorphose to the less good to
    sometime better, and often more a
    mixture of psychological states–
A small touch of lips, cheek, waist, and
    giving, alongside, Holding a gracious
    position – ah, were paradise enough –

Relationship as reflection of the needs of self
and the manner in which one's partner
helps or does not help the flowering of
this entity --

Elizabeth -- Early morning
January 17, 2009

Freely Associating...

"Manifest destiny"
"A place in the sun"
"Peace in the valley"
"The past is because it was."
"Every hurting is a small forgiveness
of our loss."
"Only flowers are what worlds merely
might have been."

Tom Dooley – we are, left late, a
dragonflower

Time wanders away slowly, fleetingly, but
the time I have in this moment, is.

Elizabeth
April, 2009

Printed in the United States
by Baker & Taylor Publisher Services